<u>A Melody & Courtney Adventure!</u>
"The (^Not So) Great Wiggle Gem Adventure."
By
Joy M. Thayer

Melody and Courtney and the (not so) Great Wiggle Gem Adventure

Joy Thayer

Published by Joy Thayer, 2023.

While every precaution has been taken in the preparation of this book, the publisher assumes no responsibility for errors or omissions, or for damages resulting from the use of the information contained herein.

MELODY AND COURTNEY AND THE (NOT SO) GREAT WIGGLE GEM ADVENTURE

First edition. October 24, 2023.

Copyright © 2023 Joy Thayer.

ISBN: 979-8223953258

Written by Joy Thayer.

Table of Contents

(This Page is left intentionally blank... Melody said so.)

Chapter 1: "A Squirmy Situation."

The autumn sun shimmered through Courtney's bedroom window. The light danced upon the walls with a jaggy stripe, caused by her window blind. With a quick glance at her alarm clock, Courtney let out a huge sigh. It was at least an hour until the morning bustle towards school. Courtney grumbled because the sunlight had awoken her early.

"*Meli... Melody*... Melody, can you turn off the *sun*, please?" Courtney said with a shake of her best friend. Melody snuggled closer to her blanket without a single blink. She was so cozy in her usual place at the foot of Courtney's bed. "*Melody! Please close the blind!*" Courtney said with a tired, frustrated tone. Melody hardly moved at her outburst.

"*No dear sir... Five doughnuts are not enough!*" Melody mumbled in her sleep.

Courtney could take it no longer. "***Okay!***" she said with a huff, pulling back her covers. Getting out of bed an hour early before school seemed like a crime. Courtney stomped across the floor with giant steps. She twisted the blind rod, closing it as quickly as she could. Then, she seemingly leaped through the air back into bed, trying to keep from fully waking.

"*Thank you...*" Melody said without opening her eyes.

"***<u>YOU BIG FAKER!</u>***" Courtney shouted, pointing at her friend.

Melody slowly lifted her sleepy head.

"*A Griffin needs a sufficient amount of beauty sleep for proper feathering,*" Melody said with a feather flip. She then carefully rested her head back on the pillow.

Courtney could only roll her eyes in disgust.

Courtney laid there for a few moments trying to reclaim her former dream. She was dreaming about jumping on clouds with Melody. She was so surprised at how bouncy they were. They jumped from cloud to cloud in an endless bounce. However, after a few minutes, Courtney sighed knowing the unwanted truth.

"*FINE! I'M AWAKE NOW!*" Courtney groaned in defeat.

She looked down at the sleeping Melody. Suddenly, she had a rascally, funny idea. "If I'm awake *an hour* before school... you're gonna' *wake up too*!" She said looking at snoozing Melody. Courtney suddenly pounced on her friend with a cat-like bound.

"I implore you... CEASE! DESIST!" Melody shrieked.

Courtney giggled with delight as she wrestled with her bestie. Melody quickly awoke and started her feathery assault. The duo fought each other hard in a morning tickle war. They giggled and laughed together in glee for what seemed like hours.

Suddenly, they stopped. The room was filled with a sweet, inviting smell.

"PANCAKES!!!" They both exclaimed.

They almost tripped over each other in a race downstairs to be first. As Courtney and Melody trotted into the kitchen, they could see their noses were correct with their prediction.

"MMMMMMMM!" They said in approval.

"You're up early! *That's a new record...*" Courtney's mom said with a smirk.

"Yeah... cause *someone* wouldn't *close* the blind!" Courtney told sarcastically, with her hand on her hip.

"*I wonder who that was...*" Melody said smiling. She stood eagerly waiting on pancakes and syrupy goodness.

"Early or not... no breakfast until you get dressed!" Mom said with authority. She held her spatula like a baton, tapping it on the countertop.

The duo looked at each other with a sigh and a frown.

"*Yes, Mom...*" they said in downcast unison.

They slunk away back upstairs to prepare for the school day.

"What should I wear today, Melody?" Courtney asked.

"I don't know... your selections are always quite *droll*... if you ask me." Melody remarked, dabbing her nose with sparkling powder. Melody had no regard for Courtney's lack of fashion sense.

"TROLL... it is!" Courtney said with a smile. She held up a shirt with a glow-in-the-dark troll doll pictured on it. She quickly put it over her head and then grabbed for her shoes.

Melody could only roll her eyes.

After a few moments of scrambling, they were both groomed and ready to feast upon fluffy perfection.

"We're ready, Mom!" The duo said together, as they took their familiar places. One by one, the heavenly golden-brown circles were stacked on separate plates in front of them. They sat gazing with their tongues wagging. They were so ready for the first luscious bite.

"Ok, dig in you two..." Courtney's mom said, almost laughing.

Courtney picked up the large bottle of syrup and began squeezing with glee.

"Not too much now... You don't need all that sugar, Courtney." Mom protested.

Courtney reluctantly put the bottle down with a frown.

"Thank you, Mrs. Emily Mom..." Melody throated in a high-pitched squeaky voice.

Courtney and her mom stopped everything and stared at Courtney with a puzzled look.

"Um... Thank you?!" Mom said slowly.

"What WAS that, Melody?! That was really weird... **DO IT AGAIN!"** Courtney said with excitement.

Melody's eyes widened in great fear. She was visibly startled by her strangeness. The odd tone reminded her of a wounded mouse, screeching in panic. She quickly grabbed her throat and tried to talk again.

"Thank you?!" Melody carefully said in her normal voice. The familiar sound made her feel once again at ease. To think that something could be amiss with her beautiful voice, was almost too much for Melody to bear.

"Your squeak is from *not closing* the blind," Courtney said with a laugh. *"IT'S KARMA!"* She said with a spooky 'Oooooooh' sound. Courtney stretched out her arms like a zombie and tried to grab Melody.

Melody dodged her arms and nervously smiled. She feared that she was somehow correct.

"Oooooh! The curse of the Squeaky Butt is upon you! Oooooh!" Courtney continued playfully.

"Squeaky Butt is *not* a curse... it's a medical problem, *MISSY!"* Melody said laughing. *"I think you have it bad..."* She continued, with sarcasm.

"Oh... really?!" Courtney said smiling, with her hand on her hip.

"Really!" Melody said with a feather flip and a lifted beak like a diva Griffin.

"Ok, you two... You need to eat and get to school! You have a big test today... *remember Courtney?*" Mom bellowed, with mom-like authority.

Suddenly Courtney's teasing stopped with a frown.

"Oh yeah... *I forgot.*" Courtney said with downcast eyes.

"◇*I shall fill your flight to school with inquisition and study!* ◇" Melody bellowed with an uplifted claw.

"*Great...*" Courtney said sarcastically with an eye roll. The last thing she wanted on the way to school is one of Melody's lectures.

"◇*It shall be exhilarating!* ◇" Melody proclaimed again with song.

"What does '*X... hill... lard... raiding*' mean? You use such *weird* words." Courtney said puzzled.

"The word is *ex-hil-a-rating*... It means '*exciting*.' It will **_NOT_** be *exhilarating* for you two if you are *late* to school!" Mom said like only a mom can.

"*Yes Ma'am...*" Courtney and Melody said together, as they both began furiously eating.

Soon, the breakfast meal was devoured. With a kiss from mom, the duo darted together back upstairs to get dressed then out the front door. Courtney and her Griffin followed a familiar path towards school.

As they strolled, Courtney sat quietly in deep thought. She did not pay attention in the slightest to Melody. Partly because she continuously talked about 'nouns and verbs.' The subject was so yucky to Courtney. The other part was she couldn't get the strange voice that Melody made at breakfast out of her head. The voice was so funny to her, yet she saw the fearful look on Melody's face. That look made Courtney feel uneasy.

"...as I was saying *Courtney*. '*S*' is sometimes added to the end of a verb when only *one person* or thing is performing an action," Melody said with pomp.

"*Yes... yes... yes... I get it.*" Courtney said in boredom.

"As in the sentence, 'Anthony **plays** the violin every day.'" The Griffin continued.

Courtney could only sit with her head in her hand.

"Now... if you said '*Anthony and Jane*' ...what verb would you use?" Melody said with a raised eyebrow.

"*What? I don't know...*" Courtney sighed in unconcern.

"**<u>YOU USE PLAY!</u>**" Melody shouted in an intense voice. She sounded like the bass-filled whoop of a professional wrestler!

Courtney suddenly sat up with considerable attention.

"**<u>WHAT IS HAPPENING TO ME?!</u>**" Melody roared in panic. Her eyes swelled like saucers! She suddenly reared back in fear, almost knocking Courtney to the ground. With a lunge, she started flying as fast as she could down the path, just inches from the ground. Melody's face filled with terror, not knowing what this strangeness was.

After several minutes of gliding, suddenly Melody stopped. Courtney again almost fell to the ground. Without warning, the Griffin began trembling and shaking. The force was great enough that leaves from nearby trees began to fall.

"*Aaaaaaaaarrrrrrrrreeeee yyyyyyyyooooooooouuuuuu ooooooookkkkkk?*" Courtney said with a very shaky sound.

All of a sudden... it stopped and Melody and Courtney colapsed on the ground.

"*Are you ok?*" Courtney said. Her head spun as she was trying to see straight.

"*Courtney...*" Melody said in her normal voice. The Griffin was so out of breath from flying and shaking. She was cautiously relieved that her voice had returned.

"*Well... we're here.*" Courtney said pointing at the school. "*I think...*" She continued. She was still very dizzy.

"*Good...*" Melody said breathlessly.

"*I need to go in... when I can stand.*" Courtney said still spinning.

"*Test...*" Melody huffed.

"*You two are so* **weird**..." Treena said with an eye roll, as she walked up to them on the school playground. She had watched the whole ordeal from the swings.

"*Weird and* **wavy**..." Courtney said trying to stand up. She swayed back and forth, stumbling into Treena's arms. Treena could only sigh in disgust.

Suddenly, the school bell rang, and Treena let her go.

"You're on your own... *dweeb.*" Treena said brushing her clothes from Courtney dust.

As Treena darted away, Courtney could only look back at her friend with great concern.

"*I'm sorry Melody... I gotta go.*" Courtney said almost crying.

"*I'll be ok... You go pass your test.*" Melody said, still lying on the ground.

Courtney walked zig-zag up to the schoolhouse door. As she opened it, She looked back at her best friend with worry. She was so afraid that something great was wrong with Melody. She had never done anything like this before. Even when she was sick with fever, it only lasted a day. Courtney feared this was something more permanent. A tear fell from her eye as she walked inside.

The entire day, Courtney could only think of her Griffin friend. She could concentrate on nothing else. Every class seemed like an eternity to her. She wanted to know that Melody was OK, so bad. She loved her best friend so much, and she could not stand to see her hurt in any way. Finally, the bell for lunchtime sounded. Courtney did not follow the herd to the cafeteria. She instead ran to the playground, looking for Melody. Courtney felt so worried because her Griffin friend was nowhere to be found.

"*Maybe she's ok and went home,*" Courtney said with a slight hope.

The regular pattern was she took her to school, returned home, and then picked her up later. However, sometimes she would randomly show up on the playground at recess. Usually, at these times, Courtney would end up feeling very embarrassed. However now, Courtney thought embarrassment was worth it, just to see her friend well. She could only stroll to the lunchroom with her head down, thinking about Melody.

As Courtney entered and stood in line, her bubble of gloom was popped. Her friend Jilly was standing next to her.

"How's Melody? I hope she's ok..." Jilly said with concern.

Courtney looked up in bewilderment.

"How did you know that something was wrong?" She said with a puzzled look.

"Everyone knows! People have been talking nonstop all day about Melody. Haven't you been listening?" Jilly questioned.

"No..." Courtney whispered.

"Well... Some think she was having a seizure this morning on the playground. Others think she's just *loco looney*. What do you say it is?" Jilly asked.

"I don't know... I'd just like to know she was ok." Courtney said, almost in tears.

"Well... Why don't you *call* her? You *DO* have a cell phone... *Dweeb!*" Treena said interrupting their conversation. She was again standing in the line, just behind them. This time it was to get ice cream.

"Oh yeah..." Courtney said in revelation, getting out of line.

"Do you want me to save your place?" Jilly said as Courtney ran outside.

She didn't answer.

Courtney frantically dialed the amulet of her best friend. She could only do so because Griffin power has natural cell phone reception, along with Wi-Fi. Courtney sighed with comfort upon hearing the voice of her best friend.

"Hello?" Melody said.

"**MELODY!**" Courtney shouted in relief.

"**COURTNEY! WHY ARE YOU SHOUTING?!**" Melody hollered back.

"Where are you? I have been so worried about you..." Courtney said in a panic.

"I am currently in a tree... holding on to a large branch." Melody said.

"**IN A TREE!?**" Courtney said, almost screaming.

"Yes. I really enjoy the view from up here. *Please lower your volume...*" The Griffin said like a librarian.

"Are you ok? Please tell me you are ok..." Courtney said with great concern.

"Yes... The Griffin is fine." Melody said, almost laughing.

Upon hearing this, Courtney's worry was lifted with ease. She could now make it through the rest of the day without breaking down.

"Have you done your testing yet?" Melody said.

"No... I still have one more class to go before... Ugh!" Courtney said in disgust.

"Always remember your adverbs and your adjectives..." Melody said, back in teacher mode.

"Yes... I will." Courtney said rolling her eyes. The last thing she wanted was to be reminded of what awaited her.

"One more thing you need...

SQUAWK!!!

SQUAWK!!!

CAW!
CAW!

CAW!!!"

Melody squealed. She sounded like the blending of a screeching eagle with a wounded crow.

She suddenly disconnected her amulet!

Courtney shook her phone in frustration, trying to call her back. She could only get Melody's voice mail. After several attempts, she could keep it inside no longer.

"WHAT'S GOING ON?!" Courtney screamed.

"You're going back to the lunch room... **THAT'S** what is going on!" The principal said, getting down on Courtney's eye level. Courtney felt scared like she was going to get detention... *or worse*. She could only comply with the Principal's wishes.

"*Yes Ma'am...*" Courtney said with her head down. She then quickly scrambled back inside, trying not to get in trouble.

"*So... did you get ahold of Melody?*" Jilly questioned, sitting at a lunch table. Like a 'good boy' he saved her a seat. Courtney sat down next to him with a peculiar look on her face.

"Yeah... I got to talk to her, but... " She said slowly.

"But, what?!" Jilly said as his eyes widened.

"She told me she was in a tree... and she squawked at me like a big bird!" Courtney said.

"*Woah...*" Jilly said dumbfounded.

"Is that all you can say?!" Courtney said with her hand on her hip.

Jilly could only nod up and down, not knowing what to say. However, After a few moments of silent thinking, he spoke.

"What if it's a joke? She's pranked you before..." Jilly said, stroking his imaginary beard.

Courtney thought carefully at Jilly's statement. Maybe all of this WAS just a joke, Courtney mused. It wasn't too awfully long ago that Melody had replaced her toothpaste with purple joke paste. It made her teeth and lips purple for two days!

"Remember the time she made you speak backward... That was so funny! And the time she caused you to burp bubbles made out of soap because you wouldn't stop to wash your hands! That was HILARIOUS!" Jilly said banging his hand on the table.

"OK... I GET IT... Sheesh!" Courtney said rolling her eyes in disgust.

After a few minutes of hard thinking, Courtney again spoke.

"Yeah... Maybe you're right, Jilly. I wouldn't put it past Melody at all to try to prank me before my big test!" Courtney said in revelation. "Melody would say it was to 'make me remember' or 'teach me a lesson' UGH! Sometimes it's tough being friends with a Griffin." Courtney continued.

All of a sudden the lunch bell rang. The children strolled slowly out the door, back to their classes. No one ever wanted to leave the cafeteria, and Courtney and Jilly were no exceptions.

"Well, Jilly.. one more class and then my *test*," Courtney said with downcast eyes.

"Don't worry... you'll do great!" Jilly said trying to lift her spirits.

"Thanks..." Courtney said with a crooked smile.

The next class seemingly flew by for Courtney. They really didn't do anything in class because they only had a substitute teacher. Melody would always refer to them as 'lesser educators' because they usually didn't give homework. Courtney, of course, LOVED them.

"*Only five more minutes...*" Courtney said to herself. She nervously looked at the clock and thought hard about what awaited her. The big test that awaited her was such a big thing at her school. It basically decided if she was to continue in her current grade level or in some way be held back. Courtney shuddered at the thought of being 'held back.' Her grades were always great. However, there was still fear in her mind that she could fail.

"What if I mess up? They could send me back to Kindergarten!" Courtney whispered with great concern. Just then the bell rang. Courtney was so surprised it startled her. It was because the clock in her class was three minutes off! She jumped like waking from a dream and almost fell from her chair.

"*Ok... you can do this Courtney,*" Courtney said trying to encourage herself. She slunk down the hallway towards her class with baby steps. All of the classmates in the hallway were seemingly going in slow motion. Up ahead, she could see the open door to the classroom. This was it... the big test that decided her destiny at Tacoma Elementary School. Courtney held her breath as she crossed the threshold into the room. On her desk was a big, brown sealed envelope. She suddenly pretended they were secret plans from a slippery-eel enemy. She believed the plans were for a bubble gum weapon, designed to surround the school in a massive bubble. After a few moments, however, her bubble of fantasy was burst by a nagging sound.

"Ok class... take your seats." Her English teacher said as the final bell sounded.

All of the students in the room scrambled for their seats. Courtney slowly sat down. She could not stop staring at the brown envelope. She knew that what was inside was very important. Courtney held her breath knowing what awaited her next.

"Ok class... you have one hour to complete your test, and make sure you use a Number two pencil to mark your answers." The teacher said.

Courtney suddenly released her breath hold and ripped open her envelope. As she read the instructions carefully, she could only think of all the things her Griffin friend had said. Melody had grilled her for answers for the last few days. Courtney began to think Melody was training her for a game show with the many questions that were thrown at her.

As the testing wore on, the students made squeaky noises. It was done with their chairs and pencils as they furiously marked their test cards. Those 'squeaky noises' made Courtney think about her friend's weirdness. She smiled thinking about all of the strange things that Melody had done today. Courtney dismissed it all as just a funny prank.

She was probably doing it to make me remember better... or just to be goofy—Courtney thought with a giggle. This certainly wasn't the first time that Melody seemingly went bonkers. Melody would always dismiss it with a Griffin-y excuse that left Courtney scratching her head in confusion. Courtney thought Melody's uniqueness was most of the time just silly or funny. However, this time seemed just a little bit different to Courtney.

Courtney marked half of her test card with answers rather quickly. Her studies with Melody had paid off. It was like she knew the answers without thinking. The reason was, from the very first mention of 'test,' the Griffin went into teacher mode for days. Courtney thought that Melody had even whispered answers in her ear while she was sleeping. However, she didn't know for sure.

Courtney quickly looked up at the clock on the wall.

'Twenty more minutes... ok, you can do this!'—Courtney thought. She was almost done with her testing. Courtney felt confident in her answers. She also felt proud in the fact that she

would probably be done first. Getting done first and knowing you are right at the same time, sounded awesome to Courtney.

Suddenly, the door swung open with a **bang!**

"THE WIGGLE GEM!" Melody shouted. She was visibly in panic mode. Her feathers were all matted and uncombed. She was covered in leaves and dust. Her sparkle was now barely a twinkle. This was so unlike Melody! She felt looking her best at all times was a necessity. To be far less than at her beautiful best, was to Melody, a great tragedy.

Everyone suddenly stopped and looked at the dirty Griffin. Courtney could only slouch down in her desk in embarrassment.

"THE WIGGLE GEM! IT MUST BE MISSING! WE MUST SEARCH POSTHASTE!" Melody again shouted as she galloped to the desk of her best friend.

"COURTNEY ADAMS!" The English teacher said sternly.

Courtney could only slouch, even more, trying to hide.

"Yes, Ma'am..." Courtney said with a hard swallow.

"PLEASE CALM YOUR GRIFFIN! THIS IS A CLASSROOM, NOT A ZOO," the teacher demanded.

"Can't this wait a few minutes? I'm almost done." Courtney whispered to her best friend.

Melody nodded silently. She then quickly trotted out of the classroom, closing the door behind her.

"Such a dweeb..." Treena whispered with a headshake.

Courtney could only roll her eyes at that statement. She once again furiously started writing. Courtney was so afraid the teacher was going to give her a punishment... *or worse.* She held her breath in anticipation. Luckily, the teacher returned to playing her cell phone game and left her alone. Courtney let out a huge sigh of relief.

Soon, everyone else in the room returned to their testing. Courtney tried to focus hard on finishing her test. However, she couldn't get rid of the words 'Wiggle Gem' echoing in her head. Melody had never acted so panicked before, much less disrupt a class. Something definitely had made her Griffin friend very afraid.

Courtney knew that whatever a Wiggle Gem was... it must be serious.

Chapter 2: "A Wiggly Adventure?"

With the sound of a loud bell, the students scrambled through the main entrance. Melody waited outside with a visible anticipation. The Griffin peered through all the children, looking for her best friend. Everyone that passed by her had strange looks upon their face. Rumors about her day of strangeness had spread all over the school. Melody dismissed their weird looks, caring only about finding Courtney. After a few moments, Courtney emerged from the crowd.

"**GET ON… WE HAVE TO GO!**" Melody immediately demanded.

Without hesitation, with a little Griffin magic, Courtney bounded on the back of her Griffin friend.

"**HOLD ON!**" Melody hollered. She reared back and then dashed with all her might past the thinning crowd of children. Courtney was amazed at the speed that Melody showed. She had never went so fast before! As Melody flew through the woods, she dodged and ducked every branch and tree.

She was a Griffin on a mission!

Courtney held on so tightly that her hands began to turn red. She was both thrilled and scared at the same time with all of Melody's twists and turns.

Suddenly, the Griffin rollercoaster stopped without warning! Courtney fell off of her friend into a large bush with a crash! Melody started spinning in circles just as fast as she was flying! Courtney had to shut her eyes from looking at her spin because it started to make her dizzy sick. After a few minutes, the Griffin stopped spinning. She collapsed and fell to the ground in exhaustion.

Courtney struggled hard to get out of the bush. Her hair was covered in leaves and twigs. Her clothes were a mess! She finally worked her way free and dashed to the side of her Griffin friend.

"MELODY! MELODY! ARE YOU OK!?" Courtney yelled with great concern.

"For now..." Melody said with tears in her eyes.

Courtney could only reach out and give her friend a hug, beginning to tear up herself.

"Please... before one of us gets hurt. Tell me what is going on? ...What is a 'Wiggle Gem?'" Courtney asked tenderly. Courtney sat on the ground next to her friend, patting her gently on the head. She was so worried. She wanted more than anything for her Griffin friend to be ok.

"I have to go... **I have to find it!**" Melody said as she quickly got up with a wobble.

She almost fell back down. Courtney continued to pat her friend, trying to calm her.

"Please... it's ok. Don't hurt yourself. Let's walk from now on." Courtney said with great concern.

Melody could only nod in agreement. She thought for a moment in silence and then spoke slowly.

"While we walk... I will tell you the story. My problems... the Wiggle Gem... everything." Melody said. She was still trying to catch her breath. Courtney could only nod and gaze at her friend as they walked side-by-side. She wanted to know more... much more.

"A long, long time ago, Griffins roamed the entire Earth. Humankind and Griffin lived together in harmony, more so than today. We would laugh and dance all over the land, spreading joy to everyone we met. And, all of the humans loved us. We would sing every morning and the humans would greet us with beaming smiles. It was such a glorious time!" Melody said with a bright smile, thinking about the long, long past. However, that smile quickly faded away.

"*But...*" Melody said with a frown.

"But what?" Courtney questioned with concern.

Melody's head sunk with bad feelings. She stopped and closed her eyes, trying to push past her visible pain. After a few moments, she began walking again and spoke.

"But, there was one human who hated the Griffins. He hated our love and beauty, and our songs of joy. He was so filled with anger and venom towards anything good, and we were his most disliked. He was a powerful wizard named Sinistral. He wanted nothing more than to silence us forever. So, with evil magic that consumed him, he cursed all of the Griffin-kind. Instead of song, he made us scary to the humans. Instead of joy... he made us jokes. Instead of dancing, we became feeble and clumsy. And as a result, we became rejected by the humans. We were driven away into the forests and woods... to be alone." Melody said as tears dropped from her eyes.

"So... that's why you have been acting so funny. **A curse!?**" Courtney said in bewilderment.

Melody slowly nodded.

"Yes... However, a great Griffin scientist named Flyter the Brave came to our aid. Through years of tireless research, She discovered a special, rare gem that could counter-act the curse." Melody said.

"The Wiggle Gem?" Courtney interrupted.

"Yes... With this wonderful news, all of the remaining Griffins gathered together to see this amazing cure. There was a grand celebration with song and dance! We were so overjoyed! We once again could be ourselves! We took the gem and placed it on a royal pedestal. The pedestal was designed by Flyter to radiate the gem and the healing it gave over a long distance, so it would help every Griffin. However, we soon realized there was a high price..." Melody said. She once again dropped her head in sadness.

"*What!? What is it!? What price?*" Courtney said with great anticipation.

"We soon realized even with research and countless attempts, we could only make the gem broadcast healing power a total of Sixty miles. Because of this, many could not go back to their former lands. *We became prisoners to the very thing that helped us!*" Melody said, turning her head towards Courtney. She had many tears in her eyes.

"But... But... But they could find more! They could place them all over the world and all the Griffins could go everywhere!" Courtney said in frustration.

"No... Courtney. Griffins have searched for centuries. We even at times moved the gem to other places in the world to look. Believe me... we looked everywhere that could be looked... but nothing. As a result, we gave up looking a long time ago. After traveling the entire world, we decided this area was the best for us to live." Melody said, wiping her eyes.

"Well... Tacoma is a really good place! And think about this thing..." Courtney said.

"*What thing?*" Melody said, still looking sad.

"*You never would have met me!*" Courtney said with a great smile.

Melody could not help herself but smile back.

Courtney grabbed her friend and gave her a huge hug.

"*Thank you... Thank you for everything.*" Melody said.

"*It was just a hug...*" Courtney said laughing.

"No... I mean **everything**." Melody said.

Courtney stood with a puzzled look at her statements.

"*I lied to you,*" Melody said, once again dropping her head.

"How? About what?" Courtney questioned.

"When we first met, I said that I was '*captivated by my thoughts*' when you found me in the shop gazing at my coffee... It was not true." Melody said with a downcast look.

"What was it then?" Courtney said, still confused.

"I was held captive by my tears. When we could not find another Wiggle gem, and we could not go home... Humans forgot about us. They forgot about our songs and our joy. And through our tears, we forgot who we were." Melody said.

The Griffin stopped and looked at Courtney again. She radiated a gigantic smile at her human friend.

"Thank you, Courtney... *Thank you for bringing back my joy and my song.*" Melody said, with tears once again welling up in her eyes. The Griffin grabbed her friend and gave her an equally huge hug.

As she let go, her back hoof started trembling furiously.

"*It's happening again... we need to go.*" Courtney said with concern.

Melody slowly nodded with a look of raw determination. She tried hard to keep herself together. After a few moments, the trembling stopped.

"**Get on! We need to get as far as we can before it starts again!**" Melody called to her best friend.

Courtney jumped on her back with a great leap… and a little Griffin power. The duo dashed through the woods with super speed. Melody was a Griffin determined! She was focused on a mission and nothing was going to turn her aside!

"*Where are we going?*" Courtney questioned like only Courtney can.

Her question startled Melody so much that it made her jump at least 8 feet in the air! Courtney squealed with delight as she held tighter. She felt like it was a carnival ride!

"**DO IT AGAIN!**" Courtney exclaimed with delight.

"PLEASE, please do *NOT* do that again! Thank you." Melody said sternly with as much breath as she could muster. The Griffin acted like she saw a ghost! Courtney could only giggle at her statement.

With a few stops for shaking and quaking, Melody and Courtney finally arrived deep in the woods. It was at this place that many other Griffins dwell. There was a crowd of Griffins surrounding the grand pedestal where the Wiggle Gem once lay. They were all standing around in great shock. Many of them had red eyes from crying. Still, others were very dirty and had their feather filled with grass and twigs from the curse's power. It was such a sad scene to look upon!

"***It is a tragedy! A travesty! A great tumult of a tempest of turmoil!***" A worried Griffin said with tears, staring at the pedestal.

"*What will we do now?*" Another Griffin said, bursting into tears.

"**We cannot find another! There is not another!**" One of the Griffin guards said in disbelief.

Sitting there watching on Melody's back, Courtney began to think deeply. After a few minutes, Courtney could not help being Courtney any longer.

"*Um... why aren't you out looking for it?*" Courtney said, jumping down from Melody's back.

"***You should be out looking everywhere, and not standing here crying and whining!***" Courtney said sternly. The many pompous Griffins were startled as such a strong statement coming from a human child. Even Melody was greatly surprised. However, the Griffin friend thought hard at what Courtney said.

"Yeah... Why are you **NOT** out looking? Instead of being **Whiney butts!**" Melody said with attitude.

"*But... but the **curse!***" One of the leader Griffins said with great fear.

"I made it here curse and all... and I did not quit and whine and pout... like all of you **cowards!**" Melody said pointing her hoof angerly at the crowd.

"You may have given up... but I have not! I will **NEVER** surrender! **I AM A STRONG, POWERFUL FEMALE GRIFFIN!**" Melody continued.

"You have been around my mom... **A LOT**." Courtney said with a giggle.

The crowd soon dismissed Melody's strong words. They quickly returned to the former mode of panic and crying.

"Sheesh! You're not going to get anywhere with these **PANSY** Griffins!" Courtney said with her hand on her hip.

"I concur... Move aside so we can look for clues! Since you **WILL NOT!**" Melody said with a strong feather flip. The duo strutted past the bawling crowd to look closer at the pedestal.

They looked it up and down for what seemed like hours. Suddenly, Courtney shouted in discovery.

"**A fingerprint!**" Courtney hollered.

"Are you sure you did not touch anything, Courtney?" Melody said with a glimmer of new hope.

"No, I did not. That's a fingerprint and you know what that means…" Courtney said looking at her Griffin friend.

"Yes! It means whoever took the Wiggle gem was **human!**" Melody said in revelation. The crowd of frail Griffins gasped. Some of them fainted and fell on the ground from the news.

"Oh my goodness… such **DRAMA!** I am glad that do not act like that…" Melody said with an eye roll.

Courtney could only giggle to herself.

"Also… knowing the gem was taken this morning… they probably live close by!" Melody continued.

Courtney suddenly had a deep thought. With a hand raise, she interrupted her friend.

"There's one over by the festive Taco stand… be sure to wash your hands." Melody stated with a hoof point.

"**NO! I don't need to do that now!** I have something to say!" Courtney said with attitude.

"Yes?" Melody asked.

"Don't get me wrong but… if this gem was so important to everyone, why wasn't it guarded?" Courtney said with a brow raise. The entire crowd turned their heads towards two trembling Griffins dressed in armor.

"*Um… um… um, we… we… took a coffee break.*" The guards said like scared children.

The entire crowd could only roll their eyes, shake their head, and sigh in unison.

Suddenly, every Griffin started to tremble like a great earthquake.

"Uh Oh! GRIFFQUAKE!" Courtney screamed, running for cover.

Every Griffin began jumping up and down. Some sounded like screeching eagles... others sounded like whales. Many of them spun in circles, while others looked very zig-zaggy with their movements. After a few minutes, the quaking and shaking stopped. Many of the Griffins began to cry once again, and retreat to their whiney places of cowardice. All Melody could do was shake her head in disgust.

"Are you alright Courtney?" Melody said, trotting to her friend's side.

"Yeah... I'm ok. I got dizzy watching everyone. **UGH!**" Courtney said, holding her head.

Melody looked back at the crowd of scaredy-griffs and rolled her eyes.

"Come on Courtney... We will not get ANY help out of them! We need to solve this mystery ourselves!" Melody said with another feather-flip away from the crowd. Courtney jumped again on her back, with a little Griffin power. Melody strutted by all of the huddled Griffins with a look of arrogance on her face.

"Well... I guess **WE** will take care of this!" Melody said in passing.

"**YEAH!**" Courtney screamed at the crowd.

"*Um... Is that all you can think of to say? I am going for **mega** sparkle points here...*" Melody mumbled quietly to her friend, as she walked away.

"*Sorry... it's been a long day.*" Courtney said.

The duo walked slowly back to town from the deep woods. As they went, they both searched for anything that looked like a clue. They looked at leaves. They spied upon animal homes. They gazed upon bushes and shrubs. They goggled upon the bottom of ponds. They studied and they gawked. They glanced and they observed. They scouted and they inspected all the way back to the town of Tacoma. Sadly, as the sun began to set there was nothing to be found.

"Well... I think the wiggle gem has gone to bed." Courtney said with a sigh.

"Yes... I must agree with you. We must stop looking for now. Tomorrow, we will search the woods more thoroughly." Courtney said with an even greater, Griffiny sigh. They walked up the steps of Courtney's home with their heads wagging. As they entered, they did not expect at all what was to happen next.

Chapter 3: "The Hunt is Aclaw"

"COURTNEY ADAMS!

MELODY GRIFFIN!

WHERE HAVE YOU BEEN!

**WE HAVE BEEN WORRIED SICK ABOUT
YOU TWO!"**

Courtney's mom and dad were standing by the door with mad looks upon their faces. After a few moments, they changed to ones of relief.

"We were so worried sick about you two! We were about to get the police involved to look for you!" The parents said in unison. They grabbed and held Courtney and Melody tightly. Tears began to roll down their faces.

"I'm sorry Mom but..." Courtney said.

"*But what...*" Mom said in a crying tone.

All of a sudden, Melody began to tremble. Her tremble quickly became a jump! The family held tighter to try to keep from falling. Melody jumped up and down frantically. She belted out a loud noise that sounded like a train whistle!

After a few moments, everything was back to normal.

"But... **that!**" Courtney announced.

The parents went "*Oh...*" together.

"You can let go now..." Melody said.

The parents released their hold with a great look of confusion on their faces.

"You might want to sit down for this..." Melody said, pointing to the couch.

They sat attentively as Melody and Courtney began to explain everything about Griffin History, weird noises, and Wiggle Gems. After a couple hours... Mom and dad had questions of their own.

"So... that's how you became to be in Tacoma? And met Courtney? **A CURSE?!**" The parents said together.

"Yes. And unless the Wiggle Gem is returned to the proper place... it will continue happening." Melody said with a downcast look.

"We need to organize a search! Make some signs! Protest in the streets! **WE WILL NOT TAKE A BACK SEAT TO OUR RIGHTS!!!**" Mom said with fury, waving her arms in the air.

"Mom... this is about Melody. *Remember?!*" Courtney said meekly.

"Oh, sorry... Habit." Mom said embarrassed.

"But... seriously we should be out looking. Get a posse together and scan the area." Dad said.

"*A posse?!* You watch too many **old** movies." Courtney said, wagging her head.

Melody thought hard about everything being said. After a few minutes, she then spoke.

"No... I think the best thing is not to cause alarm. If it was stolen, we must not alert them or they may hide it away or ship it somewhere before we can catch them. A group of people would be obvious... but a handful would not arise suspicion." Melody said.

"Like a child and Griffin crime-solving duo?" Courtney said in anticipation.

"That was what I was thinking," Melody said with a beaming smile.

The duo began to walk away to gather supplies. However, they were quickly stopped by a familiar hand.

"**Oh no, you two don't!** It's time for bed... you can look tomorrow!" Mom said with her hand on her hip.

"But... but Mom! *It's the weekend!*" Courtney argued with a foot stomp. Mom was not moved.

"*We already thought we lost you **once today**! We are not going to let you roam the streets of Tacoma **at night!**" Mom voiced with her arms now crossed.

Melody quickly complied to the voice of reason.

"She's right Courtney... we need rest and light to search. We need to go to bed." Courtney said to her friend. Courtney thought for a moment. Then with large foot stomps towards the bedroom reluctantly Courtney went.

"Goodnight Emily... Ethan..." Melody said to mom and dad. She then turned and followed Courtney upstairs. After their night rituals were over, Courtney could fight it no more.

"*Good... night... Melody.*" Courtney said with a sleepy yawn. She was soon fast asleep.

However, Melody could not sleep. Something in her mind and heart filled her with dread. She worried about the idea of not finding the Wiggle Gem.

Would she still love me? – Melody thought with a worried frown on her face. She remembered long ago when the curse first started. There were so many who said they were friends... who turned away. *Would she eventually do that to me? And her family?* – Melody thought with tears rolling from her eyes. She couldn't bear the thought of not having Courtney in her daily life. But soon, her tears could do nothing but close her eyes in sleep as well.

The next day everyone was awoken by a Melody alarm clock filled with spinning, shaking, and quaking at 7:00 AM.

"Well... at least she's accurate. I get up at this time anyway." Dad said with a laugh, trying to smooth over the situation.

Courtney, however, was not amused. Her shaking made her fall out of bed.

"*I'm so sorry Courtney,*" Melody said almost in tears.

"*It's ok... You can't help it.*" Courtney said almost in tears as well. She hated the fact that Melody was hurting. It almost broke her heart how sad her Griffin friend looked. Courtney then remembered all of the stories that Melody told of people leaving the Griffins, because of the curse. She realized that Melody probably had the same fears about her as well.

"Melody... I want you to know something. **I'm not going anywhere**. 'Best Friends' mean you are there for someone **regardless!**" Courtney said looking into Melody's sad eyes. The duo immediately embraced in a hug, filled with tears.

"*That is so beautiful...*" Dad said, crying as well.

"*Come on...*" Courtney said, motioning her dad to 'bring it in.' Everyone held each other with tears rolling from their eyes.

"You're not going to find any Wiggle Gem like that! **Suck it up and be strong!**" Mom said from the hallway like only Mom could.

"We do look kind of ridiculous, don't we? After all... it's only been a day." Melody said, almost laughing. Everyone released their hold and quickly dried their eyes.

"Ok, Melody... where do you want to look first?" Courtney said.

Melody thought for a moment.

"I think we should start again from the pedestal and work our way backward. From there we may find clues that will lead us in the right direction." The Griffin said.

After a yummy breakfast, the crime-solving team of Melody and Courtney was on the hunt. They had already found footprints leading from the pedestal. In turn, they lead away into the heart of the woods. There... the trail had seemingly gone cold.

"*We've looked in this same spot for **Two hours** now! Are you sure they came this way?*" Courtney said agitated.

"The clues have lead us here... that's all I know." Melody said beginning to be frustrated. A frustrated Griffin was not a pretty sight.

Her frustration led to anger.

"***SON OF A BLUE NOSED DONKEY!!!***" Melody yelled at the top of her lungs. Her yelling echoed throughout the woods.

"*Calm... calm... take deep breaths. Calm...*" Courtney said, almost scared at Melody's outburst. This kind of action was so unlike Melody.

"I CAN'T CALM DOWN! AS IF I HAVEN'T BEEN THROUGH ENOUGH THROUGH THE CENTURIES! NOW, I HAVE TO GO THROUGH THIS DONKEY WHO-HA, CINNAMON BUTT, PANSY APPLE STUFF AGAIN! I WON'T CALM DOWN! I JUST WON'T!!!"

"Woah... I have NEVER seen you like this!" Courtney said, ducking for safety behind a huge rock.

Suddenly, Melody started shaking and quaking again. She turned flips in the air and pirouettes in circles. She levitated and she gravitated. The trees swayed in the wake of Melody's power. This was definitely her worse one yet. However, after a few minutes, she collapsed in the dirt.

"Melody! Melody! Are you Ok?!" Courtney said, running to her friend's side.

Melody was so out of breath from the ordeal that she couldn't speak. Dirt, leaves, and twigs had been scattered everywhere from Melody's episode. Many of the woodland creatures ran away as fast as they could in fright. A mad, raving Griffin was definitely not something they saw every day.

As Melody caught her breath, something in the dirt caught her eye.

"Courtney... Did you walk over there?" Melody said slowly. She pointed her hoof directly in front of her.

"No... I was behind you. Remember?" Courtney said puzzled.

"That's what I thought..." Melody said as she stood up, brushing all of the dirt and leaves from her feathers.

"I see a whole lot of claw prints in front of me... but only one set of *human* footprints." Melody said.

"All of your jumping and wailing must have uncovered them from all these leaves! Maybe that curse is good for something... huh?" Courtney said with a smile and a giggle.

The Griffin, however, was not amused.

"It looks like the footprints lead back to town from here. So whoever took the Wiggle Gem, probably lives in town." Melody said.

"How do you know?" Courtney said with a head shake.

"♦ **GRIFFIN!** ♦" Melody sang.

The duo quickly trotted towards the heart of Tacoma. Melody and Courtney's heart soared with new hope. However,

that hope was soon put on hold, after fully knowing what
awaited them.

Chapter 4: "Tacoma Trouble"

36

Courtney and Melody followed the trail as fast as a Griffin could trot. It quickly lead them to the center of Tacoma. However, after looking around; they hadn't a clue what to do next. In the center of town, there was a fairly large park, and it was filled to the brim with people. Most weekends, much of the population of Tacoma went to the park. This was because it had three things: A large playground with a splash pad, food carts constantly going up and down the sidewalks, and Baseball.

"***It could be anyone!***" Courtney said in frustration, looking at the large crowd.

"*So many...*" Melody mumbled to herself in disbelief. The sight of so many people put fear in Melody's heart. But, after a few moments, her fears turned into reason.

"Well... I don't think it would be at the playground or the splash pad. Way too much moving around." Melody thought out loud.

"Then where should we start looking?" Courtney said.

"I think we should start by looking in the stands at the baseball fields. We might find it there..." Melody said.

"Why?" Courtney said like an inquisitive child.

"Because people are sitting down watching the game, and are not going to pay attention to what we are doing!" Melody said with a hint of attitude.

"Sheesh! Calm down! Are you going to start yelling again?" Courtney said with an eye roll.

"Not unless you bring me to it..." The Griffin said with a smile and a wink.

The duo started walking under the stands looking for the Wiggle gem. There were many in the stands due to the fall playoffs. They hoped to see a shiny glimmer from someone's pocket or purse. However, after a while of looking, they saw something else...

"EWWWWW! **Someone needs to pull their pants up!**" Courtney said out loud.

"SOMEONE NEEDS TO INVEST IN A BELT!" Melody said even louder. Many of the people in the stands started laughing at such an outburst.

"RUN! THERE'S A **CRACK** IN THE STANDS!" Courtney bellowed.

"I CAN HEAR THE **CRACK** OF THE BAT!" Melody said laughing.

Suddenly, even more were chuckling hysterically at their comments. However, one person wasn't so jolly.

"**HEY, YOU! GET OUT OF THERE!**" the groundskeeper yelled. He started running after them with a shovel in his hand. Melody scurried away with Courtney as fast as she could. Some of the people in the stands began applauding at such a sight. After a few minutes, they were on the other side of the park, away from the baseball fields.

"Do you think we lost him?" Courtney said to a tired, breathless Melody.

"Yes... no Wiggle gems either." Melody said between breaths.

"I guess the food carts and the lazy people are next?" Courtney said.

"Yes..." Melody said, still breathing hard.

Courtney and Melody slowly went up and down looking at the rows of park benches. They were all located in the center of the park. The majority sat around the grand fountain that rested in the center of it all. There were at least two hundred people in total, just sitting there. Melody though it so odd that someone would sit for hours doing nothing but staring into space or playing with their phones. The only form of real action they would take would be to reach into their purses and pockets for money when a food cart came by. They would eat and quickly go back to their inactivity.

"These people are **LAZY!**" Courtney said to her Griffin friend.

Melody could only nod up and down because she was now in full detective Griffin mode. Melody scanned each and every person sitting. She looked at their pockets and their ice cream cones. She slithered and slunk like a stealthy snake looking in bags and purses. She wanted so much to see a shiny glimmer that yelled 'Wiggle gem' to her. Sadly, after Two hours of looking everywhere, she saw nothing that suggested anyone sitting there took the Wiggle Gem. This made a shockwave of doubt come over Melody like never before.

"*Did you find anything?*" a sleepy Courtney said, rubbing her eyes. She took a nap on Melody's back after 30 minutes of looking.

"**NO... I DIDN'T! I DIDN'T FIND A BLASTED, FART CAKE, SHAM BAM THING IN THIS LAZY PIECE OF ELEPHANT DUNG! I CAN'T TAKE THIS ANYMORE! I WON'T TAKE IT ANYMORE!**" Melody said loudly with a sour attitude.

"**UH... OH!!!**" Courtney screamed. She tried to get down from Melody's back and run away to safety. However... Courtney was too late.

Melody started to spin and thrash like a large fish caught on a line. She jumped into the air repeatedly like a gazelle in a meadow. She twisted and turned in every direction imaginable.

All Courtney could do is hold on for dear life. Then suddenly... it all stopped with a great SPLOOOOSH of water going up their noses!

Melody and Courtney landed in the Great Fountain!

The lazy people suddenly stood to their feet with their phones in hand. Some started taking pictures and video. Still, others had to call their friends to tell them what happened. All of the children who were on the playground and splash pad stopped everything. The kids just had to run and see such a uni-corny site, as a soaked Melody and Courtney in a fountain.

"Well, Melody... there are all the kids. You see any Wiggle Gems?" A soggy Courtney said sarcastically.

"Nope... I do not." A very wet Melody answered.

The dripping duo slowly ascended from the fountain. They were so embarrassed! The air was filled with shutter sounds and flashes as people took more pictures. All of a sudden, embarrassing situations and dripping wet friends were the least of their problems.

"Oh no, you don't! You're not going anywhere... but AWAY!" The mad groundskeeper said, grabbing them both by the ears. The people applauded and laughed as he lead Courtney and Melody out of the main gate of the park.

"And don't ya come back for at least two months, or I'll call the police next time!" The groundskeeper said as he shook his fist at them. The dripping duo stood on the sidewalk outside the park, watching the angry man go back inside to cheers and handclaps from the people.

"*I hate this park...*" Courtney said to her Griffin friend.

"*I think I do too,*" Melody said.

After a few minutes, Melody again spoke. This time it was in a greatly defeated tone.

"*Let's go home...*" The Griffin told, almost crying.

The wet, uncomfortable sleuths known as Courtney and Melody slowly walked away with their heads down. The long walk towards home was a sad one indeed. During the entire walk, all Melody could think about was her former friends from long ago. She remembered when the curse started and how one by one, they turned their backs on her.

She loved Courtney so much! And to not have her human friend in her life was probably the greatest tragedy the Griffin could ever think of.

"*I stink,*" Courtney said disgustedly.

"*Yes... you do.*" Melody remarked with a smile.

Quickly, her smile faded away and she was met with the reality of a life without a Wiggle Gem.

"**We saw the whole town in one place!**" Courtney spoke with her head down.

"*I know...*" Melody voiced.

"**It's not here! It can't be here! There has to be somewhere else to look...**" Courtney continued in frustration.

"*I do not know... maybe we can start breaking into homes in the middle of the night looking!*" Melody said sarcastically. The Griffin's heart was losing its sparkle in the weight of such tragedy.

"*I'm sorry...*" Courtney said, sinking even lower.

"*It is not your fault. You had nothing to do with this.*" Melody said as tears began to roll from her eyes.

Just then, Courtney and Melody glanced down the sidewalk. Treena was standing there talking with some 'cool' kids.

"*There is Treena...*" Melody said sorrowing.

"**So?!**" Courtney said with a snarky tone. The last thing that Courtney wanted to hear right now was Treena's rude comments. After a few minutes, she started walking in their direction.

"*Hey, Courtney...*" Treena said while she passed. Neither Courtney nor Melody even looked up to acknowledge her presence.

"**FINE! BE THAT WAY!**" Treena said in a huff. She quickly turned and walked away angrily. As Treena stomped away, Melody looked up. A glimmer of yellowish light caught her eye.

"*Treena?*" Melody said.

"**What do you want?!**" Treena said with attitude. She turned around with her arms crossed. Now, Melody could see a glimmer of pinkish light just over Treena's head. Suddenly, Melody's heart began to sparkle.

"Please... Please turn your head to the side!" Melody said in anticipation.

Treena thought it was such an odd request, but she did what Melody wanted. Now, the area over her head was filled with purple hues of light.

"Is it?! The Wiggle Gem?" Melody spoke as she dashed to Treena's side.

"**THE WIGGLE GEM!**" Melody screamed. It was there! It was glued to the top of Treena's hair bow... but it was there! Melody jumped in delight and clapped her claws furiously.

"**YES!!! THE WIGGLE GEM!!!**" Melody squealed!

"*What's a Wiggle Gem?*" Treena said with her hand on her hip.

Suddenly, Melody picked up Courtney and Treena with her Griffin power and placed them on her back.

"**HEY!!!**" Treena yelled.

"**No time! I will explain on the way!**" Melody announced. The Griffin started running and flying with all of her might towards the woods.

After 30 minutes of bumpy explanation, Treena spoke with a snarky attitude.

"*So this rock I found and hot glued to my hairbow is what has been causing you to act **even more** weird than usual?*" Treena said.

"Yes..." Melody said, still running in the woods.

"**SO... WHY DIDN'T YOU JUST TAKE THE DUMB THING AND LEAVE ME IN TACOMA! I WAS GOING CLOTHES SHOPPING TODAY WITH MY FRIENDS!!!**" Treena yelled from the back of Melody. She certainly was not happy about their little trip through the woods.

"*When are you not clothes shopping? You even do it in school on your phone...*" Courtney said to herself sarcastically.

"Because you were the one that took it... **YOU** have to put it back!" Melody said still running.

"**WELL... I DON'T HAVE TO LIKE IT!!!**" Treena hollered.

With the fuel of pure Griffin power, Melody quickly arrived into the heart of the woods.

"**ALMOST THERE!**" Melody squealed happily. She knew this whole ugly affair was almost over.

Or, so she thought...

Chapter 5: "A Gemy, Green Mess"

Courtney, Melody, and Treena arrived to see many Griffins fretting about more than any curse could hold.

Most of them were tangled in huge vines that had grown up. Melody looked hard and discovered they were coming from the pedestal itself!

"IT'S THE SECOND CURSE!" one of the royal Griffins screamed. They were one of the only ones not trapped by green vines.

"Second curse?!" Melody said puzzled.

"Yes! The second curse! Because the wiggle gem had been taken and kept us unprotected from curses... we have been vexed with a **lesser** curse!" the Royal Griffin bellowed with tears.

Treena suddenly hopped down from Melody's back to get a closer look.

"Clematis only grows about ten feet usually... but this is **MEGA CLEMATIS!"** Treena exclaimed in wonder.

Courtney and Melody stared strangely at Treena.

"What? Can't I study plants? I look them up on **MY PHONE!"** Treena said rudely in Courtney's direction.

"So... Miss Green Thumb, how do we get rid of it?" Courtney said sarcastically, hopping down from Melody as well.

Everyone looked attentively at Treena, even the Griffins that were tangled in mega vines.

"We need a gallon of strong herbicide or a whole lot of a certain type of fungus," Treena said.

"♢ *Fungus among us*! ♢" Melody belted out in song.

Everyone looked at her and shook their head.

"Sorry... it has been a long day." Melody said embarrassed.

"Well... the fungus would take too long anyway. So we need lots of herbicide to pour in the root at the pedestal. That should take care of it quickly." Treena said.

"Where does one get such a thing?" The royal Griffin asked.

"At the local farm store. I saw it on the shelf when Courtney's mom was looking for tomato plants last month." Melody said proudly.

"Correct," Treena said.

Suddenly, a huge green vine tried to grab Courtney and Treena! Melody quickly snatched them away with her Griffin power and set them again on her back.

"*We have to go! We will be back!*" Melody yelled to the royal Griffin, as he fought with the vine.

She galloped towards town with all her might. She leaped over every rock and ducked under every tree branch with unseen precision. She was a Griffin on a mission! She felt it was her destiny to save every Griffin and free them from the curse. She was a ball of fire possessed with determination and drive!

"*CLOSED! NUH! NUH UH! THIS IS REALLY LAME-O!*" Melody yelled as she pushed on the door. The farm store had closed early that day.

"Nice use of a non-English language..." Courtney said with a smile.

"I am sorry but this is beyond proper... *THIS IS INSANE!*" Melody yelled again. Her frustration was causing her to lose her sparkle.

"Wait... I have another idea." Treena interrupted.

"*IT BETTER BE GOOD!!!*" Melody toned, like only a raving mad Griffin can.

"*Calm down... It will be ok.*" Courtney said with a head pat and a worried look. She really thought that her Griffin friend was losing it.

"We can get some from the groundskeeper at the park," Treena said.

"AT THE PARK!!!" Courtney and Melody screamed in unison. They much rather face mutant green vines than see that groundskeeper again.

"*What's wrong with the park?*" Treena questioned.

"Let's just say someone doesn't really like us there..." Courtney remarked.

Melody let out a deep sigh.

"Regardless of someone who does not like us... we need to save everyone." Melody said with a renewed sparkle.

"We need to be *sneaky!*" Courtney stated with a smile.

"Yes... I agree with you." Melody said.

The threesome trotted to the edge of the park and stopped.

"Ok, everyone down now," Melody commanded.

"Since I am the biggest, I need you to follow behind me closely." Melody continued.

Courtney and Treena nodded with hardened looks on their faces. Everyone was now in 'mission mode.' And their mission was to get the herbicide and get out alive!

Melody slunk like a jungle cat stalking its prey. She ducked behind every pole and mobile toilet in her way. She jumped over small fences and went under barriers. She moved with an intensity of a cobra! She wanted the herbicide like nothing else she had ever desired. Courtney and Treena also followed mimicking every move she made.

"HEY! I THOUGHT I TOLD YOU TWO TO STAY AWAY FROM HERE!" The groundskeeper suddenly yelled. He started running towards them with a sharpened pitchfork! Melody ducked in fright, not knowing what was to happen!

"Hey, Frank... What's up?!" Treena asked calmly.

"Why if it isn't my little friend Treena! Why are you hanging out with these two **troublemakers**?" Frank the groundskeeper questioned.

Courtney and Melody looked at each other with bewilderment.

"They are my friends... sort of. They have a big problem and only you can help them!" Treena stated.

"What kind of problem?" The man asked, putting down his pitchfork.

"They have the largest Clematis overgrowth I have ever seen! Thick vines stretching over 40 feet! We need some strong herbicide to take care of it!" Treena voiced with intensity.

Frank reasoned and thought for a moment, stroking his dirty beard with his dirty hands.

"I've got just the thing... however, you need to wear these safety goggles and thick gloves when you use it!" The man said. He handed Treena a large plastic jug, some goggles, and gloves. "Also make sure you give the jug back to me when you're done... even if it's empty. It has to be disposed of properly." The groundskeeper continued.

"Thank you so very much!" Melody said with a beaming smile.

Frank, however, was not happy.

"I still mean it! I better not see you around here again for Two months!" The groundskeeper yelled with a shaken fist. Courtney and Melody could only nod in fright.

Melody lifted everything with Griffin power and placed it and Courtney and Treena on her back. Quickly, Melody began galloping back towards the woods.

"I've known Frank for many years... we sit and talk plants together." Treena spoke.

"He seems nice..." Melody said to Treena as they trotted away.

"Nice as an electric eel..." Courtney uttered in a huff.

Soon, Melody had once again hurried with all her might into the heart of the woods.

"IT'S EVEN BIGGER NOW!!!" The threesome yelled in unison.

"Somehow... we have to get to the root at the pedestal or this stuff won't work!" Treena spoke.

"Leave it to me... **JUST HOLD ON TIGHTLY!**" Melody said with deep determination.

Melody started kicking and chopping each vine with Griffin/Kung-Fu skills. She learned them from a Grif-Fu master from long ago. She whapped and broke vine after vine in her quest to the pedestal. Her skills were definitely a sight!

"WOW MELODY! I DIDN'T KNOW YOU HAD THIS IN YOU! YOU'RE AMAZING!" Courtney said awestruck.

Just then, an unseen vine snatched Courtney from the back of her friend!

"HELP!" Courtney screamed as the plant wrapped her tighter.

"WE CAN'T STOP! WE'RE ALMOST THERE! IT WILL PUT AN END TO EVERYTHING!" Treena yelled, trying to keep Melody from going after Courtney.

Melody could only nod, knowing she was right.

After a few more chops and kicks, they could see the pedestal in front of them.

"THERE IT IS! QUICKLY MAKE A CLEARING SO I CAN WORK!" Treena yelled.

The Griffin quickly complied and chopped everything surrounding the pedestal. Treena hopped down from Melody's back with the herbicide. She frantically put on the gloves and safety goggles. But, she soon saw a problem!

"I can't get this inside the plant! I need a hole to pour in!" Treena pleaded with Melody.

"*Nuh uh! Nuh!*" Melody protested, knowing what Treena wanted.

"DO IT!" Treena demanded.

"NO..." Melody argued.

"DO IT! ALL THE STUFF IS GROWING BACK!" Treena said with attitude.

"*EWWWW!*" Melody murmured, finally getting to the root.

The Griffin reluctantly poked her claws into the root of the plant. Her claws were now covered in green, sticky slime.

"*EWWWWWWWW!*" Melody screamed.

Treena rapidly poured the herbicide into the hole made by an uncomfortable, sticky Griffin.

"*That's the whole gallon... now we wait.*" Treena said, putting the cap on the jug.

Within minutes, the vines stopped growing.

"**IT'S WORKING!**" Melody and Treena said with glee.

Rapidly, the vines curled up like a ribbon. They browned and withered with great speed.

After a half hour of waiting, the first Griffin dropped from the dying plant's grip.

"OW!" The Griffin yelled after hitting the ground.

Then all of a sudden, more Griffins dropped from the air.

"**GRIFFIN RAIN! TAKE COVER!**" Treena said, ducking behind the pedestal.

Melody, however, stood idle, under a special delivery.

"*This one is fragile...*" Melody said to herself.

After a few minutes, Courtney fell from the plant right into Melody's outstretched wings.

"**Caught Ya!**" Melody said with a smile.

The plant withered and died rather quickly. Brown vines were scattered everywhere!

"That is some good stuff." The royal Griffin said, after dusting himself off.

"Yes, it is," Treena said proudly.

Melody set Courtney down and cleared away the pedestal from all the plant debris.

"We still have one more thing to do..." Melody said looking at Treena.

Treena took off her sparkly hair bow and then removed the wiggle gem.

She slowly walked up to the pedestal and set the Wiggle Gem in place. Suddenly, the air was filled with sparkly colors! All of the Griffins could feel their strength returning. As a result, every Griffin began to cheer and applaud! The entire scene was filled with joyous singing and dancing! The Griffins were now curse-free and happy again!

However, one little girl wasn't so happy.

Treena turned around from the pedestal with a look of intense anger on her face.

"OK NOW! IF THIS STUPID GEM WAS SOOOO IMPORTANT TO YOU... WHY DIDN'T IT HAVE AN ALARM OR ARMED GUARDS WATCHING IT?!

I CAME BY HERE DURING MY MORNING JOG AND DID NOT SEE ANYONE!

THIS DUSTY OLD PEDESTAL LOOKED LIKE IT HADN'T BEEN CLEANED IN YEARS SO....

I THOUGHT THAT SOMEONE LEFT YOUR STUPID GEM HERE BECAUSE THEY DIDN'T WANT IT!

I THOUGHT IT MATCHED WELL WITH MY OUTFIT, SO I TOOK IT!

IF YOU WANTED IT SO BAD, WHY WASN'T IT PROTECTED!!!"

Treena screamed at the crowd at the top of her lungs. Suddenly, everyone looked in the direction of two cowering, scared armed guards.

"*Um... Um... Coffee Break?!*" One of the guards said nervously again.

Everyone including Treena shook their head in disgust.

"I am greatly sorry for your inconvenience, but I assure you... this will **NEVER** happen again. I thank you for your bravery and heroism. We owe you all a great debt of gratitude." The most high royal Griffin said emerging from the crowd. He regally bowed before them. In turn, the rest of the crowd also bowed before Courtney, Treena, and Melody.

The trio seemingly ignored everyone and their gratitude and pomp.

"I think it's time to go... I'm getting sleepy." Courtney said with a yawn.

"I **NEED** some food... can you drop me off at Augusto's? I can still meet my friends there." Treena asked.

"If I rush... I can still watch the NEW Mythical Creatures that comes on tonight! I can not wait! It is a **DOUBLE EPISODE!**" Melody said gleefully.

Melody picked up the duo (and the used jug) with her Griffin power and placed them on her back. She flew away back towards town, without paying any attention to the crowd of Griffins.

Soon, it was once again time for bed. They had such an adventure! Melody and Courtney were certainly very tired. However, they had to address something else before going to sleep.

"OK, You Two... **PLEASE EXPLAIN THIS!**" Mom and Dad said together in anger. They showed Courtney and Melody the latest edition of the Tacoma Gazette.

'*Hero Groundskeeper stops Vandals in the park*' was the headline plastered on the front page. It had a picture of Courtney and Melody soaked, in the fountain at the park. And another picture of Frank the Groundskeeper dragging them by their ears.

"**Honest Mom... Melody went crazy and we wound up in the fountain!**" Courtney pleaded.

"*Is this true?*" Dad asked Melody with a frown.

"Yes. Ethan Dad sir." Melody answered with seriousness.

Suddenly, their hardened looks turned into great laughter.

"**Oh Man! I wish I could have seen that!**" Dad said laughing hard.

"**...So funny seeing you two dripping wet in the fountain!**" Mom remarked, trying to keep from snorting while she laughed.

"It **was** rather funny," Melody said with a smile.

"No, it wasn't... my ear hurt for hours." Courtney protested, once again holding her ear.

Everyone chuckled and laughed about the whole situation. Courtney and Melody swapped stories about what had happened today. Mom and dad smiled and shook in laughter.

"Ok, you two. Time for bed... you definitely deserve it." Dad said.

"I am so glad you are better, Melody. I don't know what we would do without you." Mom said with a hug.

The sleepy duo snuggled together in their usual places in the bed. To go to sleep without fear of the unknown awaking them, was such a relief to both of them.

"Goodnight, Melody Sappy Claw," Courtney said with a chuckle.

"Goodnight, Courtney Leafy Butt," Melody remarked with a yawn.

With a snuggle, quickly, they were fast asleep.

A few days later, Melody, Courtney, and Treena returned to the heart of the woods.

Melody wanted to show them something...

"As you can see... They updated the old system with a few new security modifications to make sure this never happens again..." Melody announced, like a tour guide.

The pedestal was surrounded by bulletproof glass, burning lasers scanning every square inch for 20 feet surrounding, a pressure sensitive alarm system on the floor and sides, a thingy that can detect motion and people's breath for 20 feet. And... a moat of molten fire that appears when any of these things are triggered.

"What about those lame guards?" Treena questioned

"Their new duties include removing swamp sludge and scum from the bathing ponds and doing royal hoof-a-cures on a weekly basis," Melody answered.

"**Ouch!**" Courtney stated.

"Oh Yeah! One more thing, Melody... In celebration, I wanted to invite you and Courtney to a hero's party that I am having this weekend. All of the coolest kids are going to be there!" Treena said, inviting them to the party.

"Oh... Really! Wow! Thanks, Treena... that is really nice of you!" Courtney proclaimed with a smile.

"Yeah... there is going to be cake, ice cream, a band, and lots of gifts!" Treena said with glee.

"*Where is it going to be at Treena?*" Melody questioned.

"Oh... I rented a spot at the Tacoma city park." Treena said with a devilish grin.

Courtney and her Griffin could only roll their eyes in disgust.

The End... (for now.)

www.ingramcontent.com/pod-product-compliance
Lightning Source LLC
Chambersburg PA
CBHW021319160726
47994CB00004B/1516